For my mom, the likely source of my sweet tooth.

And for Zoey, the first Mythical Feasts mega-fan.

Younger Media, LLC
www.YoungerMeAcademy.com

Author: Ben Okon
Illustrator: Komal Sharma

Unicorns Love Ice Cream
Text & Illustration Copyright © 2025 Benjamin Okon

All rights reserved. No part of this publication, or the characters within it, may be reproduced or distributed in any form or by any means without written consent from the publisher.

Library of Congress Control Number: 2025901596
ISBN: 978-1-961428-24-9 (Paperback)

Younger Media, LLC offers special discounts when purchasing in higher quantities. For more information, please visit our website:
www.YoungerMeAcademy.com

Published in USA (Birmingham, AL)

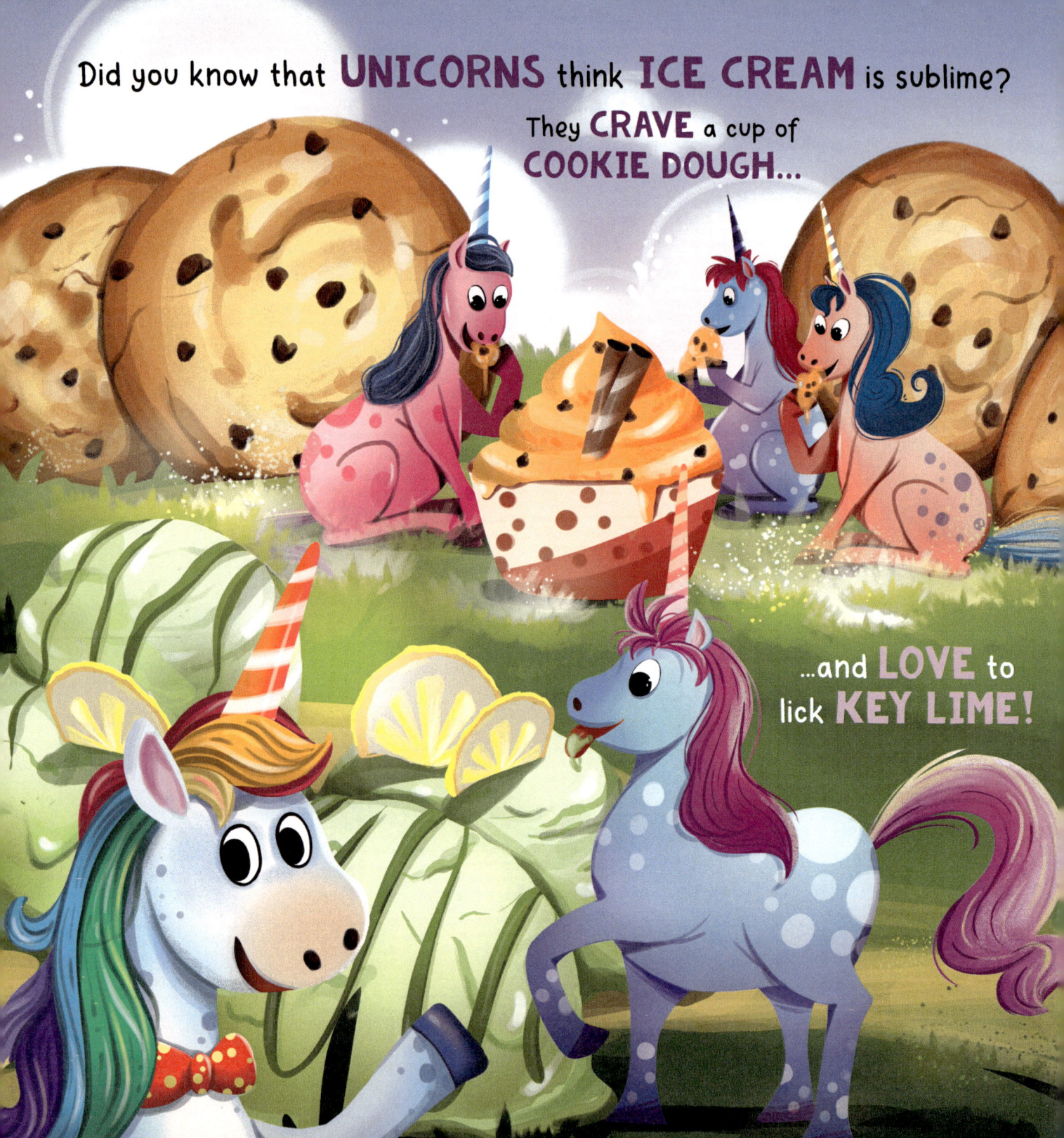

VANILLA is a **THRILLA'** (if it's topped with brownie bites).

And **SUNDAES** served on **MONDAYS** are such **ODDLY SWEET** delights!

A bowl of ice cream **CHILLS THEM OUT** and helps them keep their cool.

Can **YOU** imagine being run by such a **TASTY FUEL?**

As much as they love ICE CREAM, there's a thing they love much more!

It's RACING! They'll race anything and always keep the score!

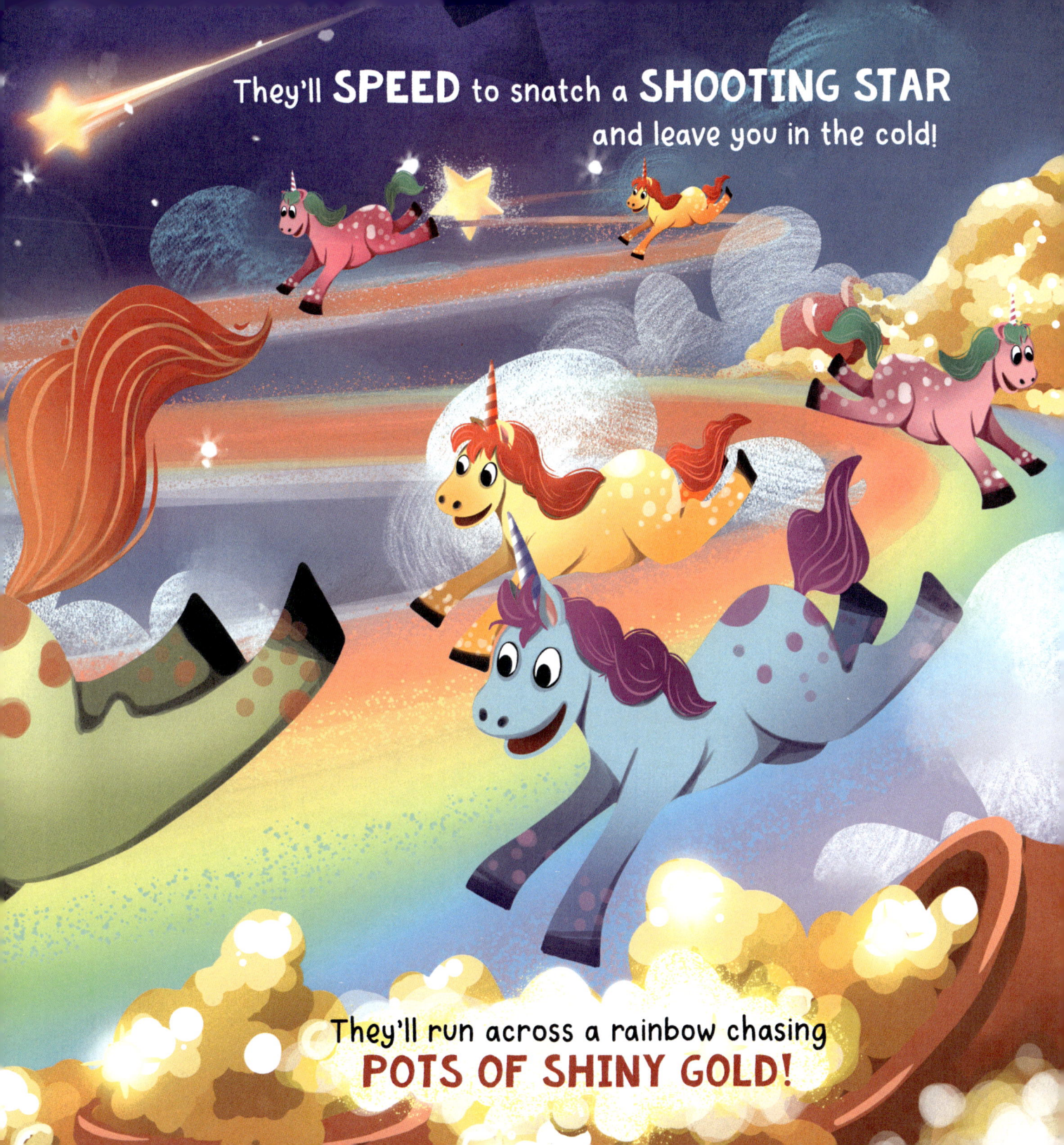

And 'corns can even **CATCH A CLOUD!**

Just **CHALLENGE** them! They will!

For **FLYING** fast like **FALCONS** is their most **SURPRISING SKILL.**

They LOVE to **RACE** with **LIGHTNING**, which they see as such a thrill!

They'll even race a rock that's **ROCK-AND-ROLLING** down a hill!

With all their MAGIC-MAKING and their RACING round the clock,

they CHOMP their ice cream QUICKLY! There's not even time to talk!

But when they **FILL** their bellies, there's **NO WAY** that they can run!

Instead, they'll **ROLL** their way back home ('cause walking's not as fun!).

I bet they'll let you ride them, if you feed them while they race! Let's **STUFF** some ice cream in their mouths until there's NO MORE SPACE!

WAIT, FRIEND! I must make certain; did you bring them any **CONES?**

'Cause if you did, the **UNICORNS** will **SURELY** whine and moan!

It's **STRANGE!**

I know, they're **UNICORNS**... and **CONES** are what they dread?!

How **COULD** they fear a **CONE** just like the **HORN** that's on their head?!

The sun then **WARMLY SHINES** to cheer the **UNICORNS** right up...

...which **MELTS** their **PRECIOUS ICE CREAM!**

That's why 'corns prefer a **CUP.**

And overcome their
FEAR OF CONES!

A rightful claim to fame!

But now they've noticed that their horns can double as a cone—
and using horns as ice cream cones is how they are now known.

FOOD FOR THOUGHT

The UNICORNS tried something new! And you probably did too (though you may not have noticed). Well done! This book followed a trickier story path and used harder rhymes and words than similar picture books. It wasn't just UNICORNS getting pushed outside of their comfort zone!

1 When you found a new word (like "Sublime" or "Dread"), how did you tackle it?
Learning new words helps build a MAGICAL vocabulary!

2 Think of a time when you stumbled on a tongue twister or unexpected plot twist. What did you do?
You can always try reading it again, or wait until later!

3 Did the book get easier the second time you read it? The third?

4 Is there something in your life that seems hard to do? Will it get easier if you try it a few times?

DO YOU WANT ANOTHER CHALLENGE?
TRY TO MAKE:

UNICORNS' ICE CREAM DREAM

Get our rhyming recipe FREE at
www.YoungerMeAcademy.com/IceCreamDream
for a delicious challenge that's a bit tougher than cookies
(No ice cream maker required!)

Made in the USA
Middletown, DE
10 September 2025

17427806R00022